P9-BZF-232

*For Jessie
and Laura*

First published in the United States 1991 by
Dial Books for Young Readers
A Division of Penguin Books USA Inc.
375 Hudson Street
New York, New York 10014

Published in Great Britain by Frances Lincoln Ltd.
Text copyright © 1991 by Matthew Sturgis
Pictures copyright © 1991 by Anne Mortimer
All rights reserved
First Edition
Printed in Hong Kong by Wing Kong Tong Co. Ltd.
1 3 5 7 9 10 8 6 4 2

Library of Congress Cataloging in Publication Data
Sturgis, Matthew.
Tosca's surprise/by Matthew Sturgis
pictures by Anne Mortimer. — 1st ed.
p.   cm.
Summary: Greatly in need of privacy for personal reasons,
Tosca the cat searches the entire house
and backyard before she finds the perfect spot.
ISBN 0-8037-0946-3 (Tr)
1. Cats—Fiction.
I. Mortimer, Anne, ill. II. Title.
PZ7.S94125To 1991
E—dc20   90-38731   CIP   AC

Tosca's Surprise

ANNE MORTIMER

STORY BY MATTHEW STURGIS

Dial Books for Young Readers *New York*

Tosca needed some peace and quiet. It was very important.

She found a warm, dark corner in the bottom drawer of a large chest. Tosca was very snug there, curled up among the sweaters.

Suddenly the drawer was pulled open. "What on earth are you doing in there, Tosca? Out you go! There's spring cleaning to be done."

At the top of the stairs Tosca was threatened by the vacuum cleaner. "*WAAAAAAAAAAAH,*" roared the horrible machine. There was no peace here.

Tosca skipped down the stairs and slipped out through her cat-flap.

She sat on the backyard steps and warmed her whiskers in the spring sunshine. Everything was quiet and still. This was much better.

Tosca stalked across the lawn, pausing only to sniff the first of the season's primroses. "*Mmmmm,*" she purred. She would have liked to have eaten one, but she really did have to find a place to lie down. And soon.

There was a warm, dry spot under the old hedge.
Tosca made a little bed among last year's dead leaves.
She was just settling herself when a loud *"wheeep,
wheeep, wheeep!"* shattered the calm. Tosca looked up.

There, right above her head, was a nestful of fledglings shouting for their dinner. *"Wheeep, wheeep, wheeep!"* At that moment their mother flew down with a fat pink worm for them.

Yuck, thought Tosca. She couldn't stay there.

Tosca walked over to investigate the large clump of reeds at the edge of the garden pond. But the ground was damp, and a large frog jumped into the water and splashed her. *"Ffrrrsst,"* hissed Tosca. She didn't like water.

But where could Tosca go? She was beginning to get desperate. She sat in the middle of the lawn, shaking the wet from her paws and wondering what to do next.

Then she glimpsed a flash of orange down by the shed at the end of the yard. She heard a gentle growl. It was her friend Roger, a fine-looking tomcat with a marmalade coat and no fixed address. Tosca strode over to see him.

Tosca and Roger rubbed noses in greeting.

"I need a quiet place to lie down," said Tosca. "I really must find one soon."

Roger understood immediately. He knew just the place for Tosca. He showed her how to climb into the garden shed by pushing aside one of the loose boards. "I often sneak in here when it's cold," he explained.

It was very quiet in the shed. There was a family of mice living in one of the old vegetable flats, but as you can imagine, they didn't make a sound.

Behind the tottering stacks of flower pots and seed trays there was a pile of old sacks. Tosca climbed onto them. It was all she could have wished for; it was warm and quiet and hidden away.

Night fell. An owl sat hooting in the old oak tree behind the shed. The family of mice crept out of their beds as quietly as they could to see what was happening.

The next morning the door of the shed was opened. Sunlight flooded in.

"Ah, there you are, Tosca! We've been looking for you everywhere. And look! Oh—Tosca—how wonderful. You clever cat!"

Proud Tosca.